Computer Virus

by Christopher Stitt

illustrated by Lew Keilar

Characters

Vinnie

Mary,
Vinnie's mum

Dr Hacker

Contents

Chapter 1
The Sniffles

Chapter 2
From Bad to Worse

Chapter 3
Slimy Green Stuff

Chapter 4
Dr Hacker

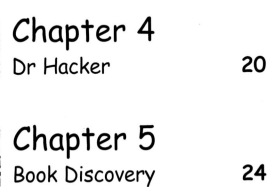

Chapter 5
Book Discovery

Chapter 1 — The Sniffles — 4

Chapter 2 — From Bad to Worse — 8

Chapter 3 — Slimy Green Stuff — 12

Chapter 4 — Dr Hacker — 20

Chapter 5 — Book Discovery — 24

Chapter 1

The Sniffles

Vinnie raced in the front door. His bag skidded across the living room floor.

"What's going on in here?" Vinnie's mum stood in the doorway, hands on her hips.

Vinnie walked over and picked up his bag. "Sorry, Mum. I'm in a bit of a hurry."

"Your bag belongs in your room."

Vinnie smiled sweetly. "Sure, Mum. I'm going to do my homework anyway."

"What about a snack?"

"I'm not hungry."

Mary stood in shock as she watched him run up the stairs. Vinnie was always hungry after school. She knew something was wrong.

Vinnie threw his bag on his bed and took out his assignment. "Hope I can get this done tonight. I'm in big trouble if I don't." He turned on his computer. The screen was blurry. Something was wrong. It normally warmed up more quickly than this.

The screen finally cleared and a green face appeared. It looked sad and unwell.

The screen groaned. "Turn me off, please."

Vinnie couldn't believe it. "Did you say something?"

"Turn me off."

"I can't, I have homework to do."

The computer screen crackled. "Do it tomorrow."

Vinnie panicked. "I have to hand it in tomorrow."

"Not possible," wheezed the computer. "I've caught a virus." The computer turned itself off.

Vinnie thumped the desk. "No. You can't do this."

Chapter 2

From Bad to Worse

There was a knock on Vinnie's bedroom door.

"I'm busy, Mum."

Mary peered inside. "Are you feeling sick?"

"No, Mum. I have a lot of homework to do."

Mary walked over to her son. She looked at Vinnie's assignment. "You have to do all this in one night? I'm going to ring the school."

Vinnie hid the sheet behind his back. "It's not that bad."

"It's a big assignment on a whole country in just one night." Mary waved her finger. "That's too much."

"Please don't ring the school," begged Vinnie.

"When did you get this assignment?"

"Well ... um ... it ... was about two weeks ago."

"Two weeks!" exploded Mary. "Why haven't you started it yet?"

"Football finals."

Vinnie's mum nodded. "Right! If you don't hand this assignment in on time, and get a good mark, there'll be no football next season."

Vinnie's bottom lip dropped so far it almost hit the floor. "But Mum ..."

"Don't 'but Mum' me. You'd better get to work." Mary stormed out the door.

"My computer has a virus. It won't work."

Mary laughed. "Nice try Vinnie, but I don't believe you."

Vinnie ran to the computer. "I'll show you."

Mary kept walking. "Do it tonight, or no football."

This was going from bad to worse.

Chapter 3

Slimy Green Stuff

Vinnie turned the computer back on. The screen fizzled. The sick face appeared again. "I told you to leave me alone. I'm not well."

Vinnie sat in his chair. "Just a little assignment. Nothing too big. Ple-e-e-e-ase."

The computer coughed. "My hard drive is all clogged up. My motherboard has aches and pains. I've got mucus in my modem."

Vinnie clicked an icon. "I have to surf the net. I need to find out all about France."

The computer turned a brighter shade of green. It looked like it was going to be sick. "Don't talk to me about surfing."

The disk drive flew open. It was dripping with slimey green stuff.

"Yuk! What is that?"

"I told you I had mucus," the computer sniffled.

Vinnie sat back in his chair. His mind was racing. He was going to fail for sure.

No! No way was he going to miss out on football.

"What am I going to do?" Vinnie yelled at the computer. "I'll fail because of you."

"I'm very sorry," coughed the computer. "I didn't choose to catch a virus."

An idea flashed into Vinnie's mind. He had seen an ad for a computer doctor. But where had he seen it?

Vinnie dived under his bed and rummaged through the mess. He slid out holding a computer magazine in his hand. Vinnie thumbed through the pages. "Here it is."

Vinnie tore the ad from the magazine and crept downstairs. There was no sign of his mum. As he reached for the phone, it rang.

Vinnie almost hit the ceiling. He ran back to his room. Mary answered the phone and then hung up quickly. Vinnie heard his mum walking up the stairs. He sat in front of the computer.

Mary opened the door. "I have to pick up your sister from ballet. Keep up the hard work." She closed the door.

This was Vinnie's chance. His mum usually took about half an hour to pick up his sister. Vinnie leapt down the stairs.

Chapter 4

Dr Hacker

Vinnie ran to the phone. He pulled the ad from his pocket and dialled the number.

"Hello," said the voice on the other end of the line.

"Are you Dr Hacker?" asked Vinnie.

"That's right."

Vinnie explained his problem.

"Never fear, young Vinnie. I'll be there in a flash," said Dr Hacker.

Vinnie hung up. Smoke filled the hall and a flash of light blinded him. Vinnie rubbed his eyes.

Dr Hacker waved away the smoke. "Show me your sick computer."

Vinnie asked, "How did you do that?"

"No time to give away my secrets, young Vinnie. Just take me to the patient."

Vinnie showed his computer to Dr Hacker. "Hmmm... doesn't look good," Dr Hacker sighed. He brushed back his frizzy hair. Dr Hacker took out his stethoscope and put it to the computer screen. "It doesn't sound too good either." He shook his head.

Chapter 5

Book Discovery

Dr Hacker examined the computer. "Oh, Doctor," moaned the computer. "I feel terrible, just terrible."

Dr Hacker turned to Vinnie. "I've found the problem, young Vinnie."

"Can you fix it?"

"I can."

Dr Hacker cleared his throat. "Your computer has byte bronchitis."

"Does it need medicine?" asked Vinnie.

Dr Hacker fumbled in his bag and pulled out a bright blue bottle. The computer's disk drive opened. Dr Hacker poured the blue liquid inside.

Vinnie took the bottle from Dr Hacker. "Can I use the computer now?"

"No. It needs to rest for at least two days."

Vinnie dropped the bottle. "Two days! I need to do my assignment by tomorrow."

"What is this assignment?" asked Dr Hacker.

"I have to do a project on France," Vinnie whined.

Dr Hacker closed his bag and shut down the computer. "I have an idea. Do you have any encyclopedias?"

Vinnie stared at Dr Hacker. "Um... I think so."

"Use them." And before Vinnie could say anything, Dr Hacker vanished in a puff of smoke and a flash of light.

Vinnie was sitting in the family room when his mum and Lara arrived home.

"What are you doing?" asked Mary.

"I'm using the encyclopedias." Vinnie showed his assignment to his mum.

"It looks good."

"Why aren't you using the Internet?" asked Lara. "It would be much quicker."

"I thought I'd give the computer a rest," said Vinnie, "and all the information I need is right here."

Vinnie looked happy when he came home from school the next day.

"How did you go?" asked Mary.

Vinnie gave her the assignment. "I got the best mark in the class. Guess you'll have to buy me those new football boots after all."

assignment
a school project, task

icon
a small picture on a computer screen which links to a program

modem
the equipment that links a computer to the telephone line

mucus
sticky substance made in nose

rehearsing
practising

rummaged
searched for something by
moving things about

skidded
slid without control

stethoscope
a doctor's instrument for
listening to the chest

virus
a germ that makes you sick;
a bad computer program that
causes damage

wheezed
breathed with a whistling sound

Christopher Stitt

Most children know more about computers than a lot of adults.

- Adults probably think a modem is what you did to the lawn when it grew too long.
- If you asked them what a mouse pad was, they would tell you it's where Mickey lives.
- I know a lady who thought the Internet was something you used to catch fish.
- We know that a diskette isn't a female disco dancer.
- And it's a good thing that your computer won't sneeze mucus all over you if it ever caught a virus.

Lew Keilar

I had to call someone ! I think it was urgent!!

Do YOU remember who Vinnie had to call ?